Bristol To Ca

A

Family War Story

Author

Paul Thomas

Preface

No doubt World War II or Bristol history experts may take exceptions to some of the things in this book. It is based on the stories I think my father, uncles and aunt told me when I was six or seven, some sixty-five years ago. So my memory may well have failed or faded.

In addition, they told me them about ten to eleven years after the war ended and fifteen years since most of the events happened; so their memories may have been a bit jumbled as well.

What I do remember is the tone of their voices when they told the stories. That tone was fear, relief at surviving and a resolution to never be in the same situation again. They never retold the stories to me later in my or their lives. They were either in their late teens or early twenties when the war started. When it was over even the eldest was not even thirty.

The stories were not told in the order that they appear in this book. I have ordered them to create a flow.

Reg

Reg had first heard the air raid warning siren about 10 minutes before he reached the ground, the last ten rungs of his ladder were a blur in his mind. As he reached the ground his legs were already running in the direction of the air raid shelter. In the distance flashes lit up the night time sky. He dived in to the shelter doorway. Warden Welsh Jones, why is it we think up the most obvious nick names Reg thought, ticks his name on the sheet and told him to go as far down as he could: "there are more to come", the Cardiff accent growled at him.

Reg sat on the wooden bench and tried to marshal his thoughts. The flashes looked to be towards his home city: Bristol. The flashes did not tell him where or how bad the situation was. This was the first time that Bristol had been attacked. Reg knew of the damage to London and Portsmouth, bombing aimed at both people and ports. Those in Bristol had fortified themselves with the view that Bristol was further away, maybe too difficult for the Luftwaffe to reach. Tonight proved that belief to be false.

Reg had been born in 1918, the immediate consequence of his father Fred's return from service in France. Fred had not shot anyone, nor had he been shot: shot at yes, but no hits. He returned a man who had known fear and how bad it was to be away from home, your wife and family during war. He had quickly found a job on the docks at Bristol and had quickly moved to Avonmouth as that grew in the post World War 1 boom. As was the way then, Fred "organised" a job for Reg when he reached school leaving age: 15 in Reg's case. Reg liked the dock environment. Many of his fellow workers were good to work with and were also “sound” drinking, dance attending and Bristol Rovers supporting mates.

Just before the war started he had met Nelly and a vibrant, sometimes stormy, but always loving relationship started. This progressed into a marriage brought on by the declaration of war. They probably did not have to rush as by this time Reg was a highly skilled dock worker and was therefore placed in a “reserved occupation” i.e. his initial war effort would be as a dock worker handling the necessary cargos that would keep the British war effort going. Well connected through his father and the loss of those more senior to other war roles meant that Reg’s work was essentially that of a senior crane driver. He wore his allocated uniform with pride, as did all of his brothers.

As he sat, head in hands, he tried to recall the flashes he had seen; where had they been exactly? Were they bomb explosions or incendiaries? Did he even know the difference, yes he had heard about the incendiaries used on Portsmouth, but the war effort meant that that sort of "education" was not happening. With the exception of very big events most of the limited official news was about things that might be seen as "wins".

Harry Clarke, known as Nobby, sat next to Reg. "What do 'e think Reg, bloody Jerry must have missed London." "No" Reg said, 'this is no accident" and then adding as an after thought: "He is after the aeroplane factory or trying to deny the troops their fags by taking out WD and HO." WD and HO Wills were cigarette factories in Bristol. Before the war tons and tons of leaf tobacco had passed through the Bristol docks. Further down the shelter Billy Dean called out that he thought it proved Hitler supported City because he had guessed the bombs were falling on the Rovers ground at Eastville. Reg called back: “the only way City could win was by devious means, but not even City would sign up to Hitler”. A hesitant ripple of laughter and/or mumbled agreement rang around the shelter. Silence returned as each there concentrated on their own thoughts and fears.

Reg screwed his eyes tight shut and tried again to position the flashes, were they near Fishponds, Filton, or Knowle? He decided that they were near St Paul’s or may be in the Basin. If he was right his immediate family were safe: He knew that his sister, Doris might be out with medical teams, but somewhere in the back of his mind he remembers that she should have been in Southmeade hospital doing night duty, so she should be safe.

Not that Doris was ever truly safe. She was a year or so younger than Reg. She had excelled at school, but wanted to be outside doing things, book work and exams where never going to be her existence, she was going to be "about town". Had it been possible at the time, Doris would undoubtedly have been one of those girls that signed up for front line battle duty; firing guns was definitely what Doris wanted to do. The outbreak of war was to be Doris' chance, however Fred and Elsie worried that Doris would get herself killed at the first engagement such was her determination to be "active". Weeks and weeks of arguing, ranting, raving, door slamming, meals not eaten in protest ended with an uneasy truce. Doris could join the Nursing Corps and could, as she gained qualifications, progress to front line care with the family's support. Hence the night duty as part of her training.

Reg should have worried, because once news of the air raid and the news that there were casualties Doris was away from the night duty (a colleague said she could cope). So she was jammed in an ambulance on its way toward St Paul's to tend that injured.

The air raid lasted about an hour or so, nothing had fallen in the immediate area of the shelter. Once the "all clear" sounded the dock workers emerged slowly. They fanned out to their various work stations, but walking slowly searching every inch for unexploded bombs, shrapnel, debris and a hundred other dangers, real or imagined. Later in the war this care would disappear as everyone became "familiar" with bombing. Reg started the long climb to his cab in the crane. As he ascended the ladder the glow that was Bristol on fire became clearer and clearer.

It took no more than another 20 minutes to unload the grain sacks. The signal from the foremen confirmed that the unloading was complete. Reg shut down the crane, noting as he did so that in his haste during the air raid most switches had not been in the safe positions. Without the pressure of the attack Reg rechecked all the switches and dials: OK to decamp he thought. Normal time shut-down took about 20 minutes to be completed and with feet on the ground, so the 10 minutes earlier in the day had shown Reg how frightened he had been.

Doris

Doris stepped out of the ambulance a short distance from the road block set up to give the firefighters, medics and police room to work. Her uniform helped her pass the part-time policeman responsible for controlling entry. For a moment Doris just stood and starred at the scene in front of her.

Three houses that had obviously been joined were well alight, the heat was intense. The flames lit the road and the remaining outlines of the three buildings, but combined with the water plumes from the fire hoses they colluded to make every thing else dark and indistinguishable.

Doris was broken out of this trance of horror by a lady's voice calling for help."Nurse, nurse, help my baby is burnt, she needs help". Doris stopped, fearing the worst that the baby was beyond saving. She moved towards the lady, who was soaking wet and holding a soggy bundle in her arms. The woman's face was black and bright red on one side. In this light it was impossible to see if this was the early signs of a serious burn, bleeding cuts or just that she was very flushed.

Doris bent down to look at both the woman and her child. The child was still, very wet but breathing, albeit very laboured. She tried to reach out to hold the baby, but the mother resisted swinging away from Doris. "You not going to take here away", the woman said. "No" Doris replied, "I need to examine her to work out what is best". Slowly the woman turned back toward Doris. Without moving to take the child Doris pushed the wet cover over the side of the baby's face. The marks on the child's face did not look too deep, Doris guessed that it would blister, but with ‘standard treatment” there would be very little lasting damage.

As Doris released the child back to the mother's care her eyes noted the glistening mark across the woman’s fore and upper arm. This, Doris guessed, was far more serious than the marks on the child. She needed to act, but in all the confusion, what? "Where is the ambulance on which I scrounged the lift? she had thought. It was nowhere to be seen. She thought "I need to get the heat out of that burn". The soaking cover of the child offered an immediate option, but how to get is from the baby to the woman was clearly going to meet will strong resistance.

Doris said to the woman; “the child has a burn, it is not serious, but I am worried that it may start shivering either for shock or cold.””

The reason for the shivering is important, so I would like to eliminate cold as the reason, so can you take the wet covering off and put my jumper around the child. My jumper is dry". "Put the cover over your arm, we may need it again."

Slowly the woman did as she was asked. Doris noticed the woman wince as the cloth touched her arm. The child stopped crying, probably sensing the jumper as something different: the crying returned after a few minutes, clearly the child's burn was hurting. Help was needed and quickly. Doris' attention returned to the scene around her. The buildings were still on fire, possibly the flames were not as high as they were, but the heat from the fire and the steam from water used to douse the inferno seemed unchanged.

To the left of the last building Doris saw the ambulance driver that had given her the lift to this hell-hole. " Daz, Daz, Daz" she shouted as loud as she could, desperate to be heard over the cacophony of noise: Fireman, buildings burning, people shouting, babies crying, pumps, distant bangs as more bombs exploded.

For a moment it looked as though Daz had not heard her, but he had. Taking a few minutes to work out where the call had come from he walked ("do not run, you are more likely to trip" echoed from his training) quickly in the direction of Doris' call. Two or three minutes of dodging bricks, fire-hoses and people got him to Doris' side. She explained the situation and they agreed, hospital for both the woman and the child.

The ambulance was just behind Doris, why she had not seen it she did not know. It had been no more that 50 feet away. True it was in the dark and the other side of the barrier, but it was exactly where she had left it! No matter, the two were loaded and Daz set off back to the hospital. Doris stayed to help others.

Some time in the early hours of the following morning Doris walked back to the family home to fall into bed, unwashed, exhausted and about 4 hours later, hungry.

She was back on night duty the following evening, on the dot at 7 pm. Not without repercussions: called into the matron's office and given a stern warning about leaving her post on the ward. She never saw Daz again. He was assigned to an ambulance station on the other side of the city and after the war moved to Devon.

Thirty-three years later, at the back of the crematorium sat a smartly dressed woman with a elderly lady. If you looked carefully you could see a scar on the cheek of the smart lady. The elderly lady clearly had a badly marked left arm. At the moment when the celebrant invited those to quietly say their own farewells to Doris, the two ladies simply said; “thank you, and we thank you every day we live”.

Reg

At the foot of the ladder, Reg joined up with Spider Webb and Bob Law to find transport back to Bristol. They wandered to the main docks bus station, discussing the night's events as they went. The consensus was that "Jerry had made a serious error taking on the historic city of Bristol. It's inhabitants would not be ground-down, they would simply build more aircraft, deliver more and more war supplies and send more young men to fight". Reinforced with these thoughts they waited for transport to the city.

Damaged roads, fires and diversions had thrown the bus schedule into utter confusion and this might have been the first clue to Reg and his friends, just how bad the aftermath of the attack was. Eventually a bus arrived. Reg peered at the non-illuminated destination board: not illuminated because of black out rules. City Centre it said: "That'll do" they chorused. " It might do" the driver said " I doubt we will get there" he added. More cold shivers ran down the backs of the dock workers. "Happy Larry this driver" some thought.

The driver waited for about 15 minutes before shifting into gear and setting off. The journey normally took about an hour, but with headlights blacked out, so just a pencil slim beam lighted the way forward, it took about an hour to reach Westbury-on-Trim; less than half way. Reg was beginning to be concerned, although they had finished early, it was now more than an hour after he would normally be home. At least Nelly was at the family home so Dad and Mum would be there, hopefully to calm any fears. Clearly Reg did not understand that two worried women together create scenarios much worse than the most skilled thriller writer could fashion. Fred had tried to quench the stream of "what could have happened?" but "he is ok and on his way" or "but the bombs may have caused diversions and delays" wore thin and ineffective after the third time.

The bus reached Redlands about 40 minutes later to be met by a police road block. After some debate the driver said he was going to try to get through Clifton and follow the Avon Causeway. For Reg and Spider this was completely the wrong way: "No option but to walk

Reg" Spider surmised. "Yep, Let's get going" Reg said. About an hour later, having the way lit by the reflections from the fires, accompanied by the distant noise of fire fighting, fire engine and ambulance bells, Reg and Spider had gone their separate ways home.

Reg was "indoors" some time later: three, maybe four hours later than normal. Nelly hugged him and then immediately demanded to know "why he was so late ?" Reg explained all that had happened. Conversation came hard. The family sat in the front room illuminated by the glow of the fires still raging in the city. Each had their own thoughts: too frightened to voice them. "What had their world become?", "how could they stay safe in the mayhem of night bombing?" " Would they or the other members of the family survive?". "How would they deal with the dreaded call?"

The realisation of what had occurred suddenly exhausted them and they were soon making their way upstairs. Reg and Nelly climbed into bed and simply held each other terrified, but at the same time revelling in their personal closeness. Clearly the exhaustion passed because that night their son Malcolm started his life.

Hours after Reg and Nelly “retired” Doris came home. Elsie who had gone to bed and then got up to wait for her, demanded to know what had happened and then "why Doris had been so irresponsible". Fred, who had got up when he heard the key operate the front door, patted her on the shoulder. The house eventually fell silent about 5 hours later than what had previously been normal: still illuminated by the city fires. It might have been quiet, but Fred and Elsie looked out of the bedroom window starring at the fire glow and fretted about the future for their four children.

Ron

Ron stared at the turbulent sea. His first crossing from Canada to Bristol. So far the escort mission had made him sick: whether it was the continuous course changes, the smell of marine diesel below deck or most of all, the fear as they neared the United Kingdom shores of a U boat attack dumping him in that cold, black evil water; he did not know. Just weeks before he had been "safe" training in Lossiemouth and before that he had been a fire watcher at the Filton Aircraft factory waiting for call-up.

Seventeen, halfway through his electrical apprenticeship at Wills, the outbreak of war picked him up and threw him into the Fleet Air Arm. Ron did not understand the logic that placed a youth with no sea, not even sea-side experience on a warship. Yes they had given him training Cornwall, Blackpool and Lossiemouth, yes they "allocated" him to electrical engineering, but so far duty appeared to be mostly staring at the sea for signs of U-boat periscopes, sleep and the odd task to somehow repair the unrepairable. Fleet Air Arm surely meant naval aircraft not escort vessels. Ron was convinced he would not survive this ordeal: but he would.

HMS Arabis was newish, it had been built and commissioned quickly as the Navy tried to create a force to combat the German naval threat. He had joined the ship about four weeks before. A high speed (16 knots!!!) dash across the Atlantic to Halifax. No shore leave just servicing, training and sleeping in bunks that must have been specifically designed to be so uncomfortable that sleep became induced purely and only by exhaustion.

This crossing escorted about 25 freighters mostly at 10 knots. It was the first time he had experienced the zig-zag, circling back and the bucking seas. It really disorientated him no matter whether he was above or below decks. Above decks at least the air did not smell of humanity, fuel and fear: just fear.

Ron had been a lively student at school, books rather than sport. In post-war England, Ron might well have had the student support (financial and pastoral) to succeed in further education, but his route from school was to be an electrician via a standard apprenticeship. He had proven to be a quick learner and was considered a very bright prospect. Ron, as all 16/17 year olds, had developed friendships at school that had been maintained into work and reinforced through Friday and Saturday night pubs and dances. The outbreak of war and conscription meant that his closest friends were all "dispatched" to the Army or the Air Force or the Navy. They really had no idea of what was to befall them. Most were convinced that they were more likely to do damage to their own side than make a war winning contribution: but to serve they must, and do their best they would.

Staring into the darkness, looking toward the vast Atlantic ocean, all Ron could see was waves, waves and the odd white cap. Stan, also a seventeen year old on his first crossing, was "stationed" 10 or so feet closer to the front ("Sorry Bow; I must get to grips with the naval language" Ron thought). Stan was from a small town close to Bath. So besides being in the same bunk area, they at least had something common to talk about: the girls from Bath.

Stan was waving and pointing to the sky. What the hell was he on about Ron thought. It was nearly impossible to hear each other above the sound of the wind and the sea. Ron saw what Stan had seen just as the ship started a very tight turn. The heal over was excessive Ron and Stan desperately clung on to the side rail. The forward gun crew ran past them. How the non-conscripted crew moved around the ship so effortlessly confused Ron and Stan: They thought that they would never achieve such skills: but they did.

The ship levelled and seemed to be steaming directly towards where the aircraft had been. Ron saw the gun elevate into a firing position. Ron looked sky wards and saw the aircraft backing away and diving down. He glanced back at the gun which was trying to track the aircraft. Aircraft recognition had been part of his sketchy training. That was a Hudson he thought: “One of ours” he shouted. The shout lost in the noise of the sea, the wind and a gun crew totally focussed on defending the ship from a cruel enemy.

“I need to tell them it’s one of ours” Ron shouted to Stan. A second shout swallowed up by the sea and the wind. Bracing himself Ron charged forward to the gun. The ship bucked and banked as he set off. Ron collided with hard metal objects, bounced off the guard rails and stumbled forward. Grabbing the protective shield alongside the gun Ron swung himself in amongst the gun crew. He knocked two to the deck. The “naval language” from the two on the deck was ripe: many phrases Ron heard for the first time. Ron bellowed “ It is a Hudson, one of ours”. “Are you sure?” the remaining up-right gunner said. Not a time to hesitate Ron realised. “Yes” he bellowed again. The gunner grabbed the microphone system and gave the Bridge Ron’s identification. “It is dark are you sure?” Was the bridge officer’s response. Sensing Ron’s honesty, intelligence and skill, without a break, Joe Johnson replied “Yes”. “Gun crews continue to track, but do not engage unless fired upon” was the command over the tannoy. The two sprawling gun crew members recovered their composure and became a team again. One of them with a Newcastle growl said: “You had better be right or we are all dead meat”. Ron was sure, but now the cold sweats started. Had he been right? it was only a glimpse. Maybe the aircraft was lining them up for the kill.

The noise of the aircraft was loud now, both guns swung their aim to the port side. The Hudson appeared from out of the darkness. A crew member waved in recognition and it backed away towards its base in Ireland. Ron breathed a sign of relief. The aircraft crew had little knowledge of how close they had become to being casualties of friendly fire.

The aircraft type meant that they were nearly at the end of this escort. Yes, the submarine threat was still there, but somehow Ron felt they were close to job done. Indeed about 12 hours later HMS Arabis turned south, back down the Irish Sea, still scouting for submarines, whilst the merchant ships made their way into Liverpool, earlier a few had "peeled off" destined for Bristol or Cardiff.

Surely Ron would soon get some shore leave, simply to stop feeling this sick. The answer: no. Ron thought he would have two days while the ship was replenished and checks were made, but he became one of those doing the checking switches, dials, cables and ducts.

Peggy

About 6 months earlier Peggy Williams had stared at the order form in front of her. Six Bristol Beaufighter aircraft in component parts to be boxed for overseas transportation. The Bristol aircraft company was flat out building as many aircraft as fast as they could. The aircraft were urgently needed to build the airforce capability.

Peggy had joined the company about a year before war was declared. She joined as an administration assistant, but accuracy with numbers and a temperament that placed correctness way above speed meant that she was rapidly moved to the order department as a full administrator. Her boss Richard Davis trusted her, actually he left her to organise the paper work to and from the production floor and to the facility at Weston-Super-Mare. This order was new, she needed to speak to Richard.

The Bristol Type 156 Beaufighter was developed by the Bristol Aeroplane Company. It was originally conceived as a heavy fighter variant of the Bristol Beaufort torpedo bomber. The Beaufighter proved to be an effective night fighter, which came into service with the Royal Air Force (RAF) during the Battle of Britain, its large size allowed it to carry heavy armament and an early airborne interception radar without major performance penalties. The Beaufighter was used in many roles; receiving the nicknames Rockbeau for its use as a rocket-armed ground attack aircraft and Torbeau as a torpedo bomber against Axis shipping, in which it replaced the Beaufort. In later operations, it served mainly as a maritime strike/ground attack aircraft, RAF Coastal Command having operated the largest number of Beaufighters amongst all other commands at one point. The Royal Australian Air Force (RAAF) also made extensive use of the type as an anti-shipping aircraft, such as during the Battle of the Bismarck Sea. The Beaufighter saw extensive service during the war with the RAF, the Fleet Air Arm, the RAAF, the Royal Canadian Air Force, the United States Army Air Forces, the Royal New Zealand Air Force, the South African Air Force (two squadrons) and the Polskie Siły Powietrzne.

"Richard, you passed me this order, but it is not normal. We usually supply spares in soft packaging, the military box it, if they need it" Peggy said. "Well normally the military move the spares, but in this case we have been asked to get it ready and transport it" Richard replied. "Where to?" Peggy asked. "I cannot tell you at the moment. Get it boxed and then I will tell you where to send it" Richard responded. Peggy absorbed Richard's response and wondered "what is the truth, why is the ministry or someone else doing this? Is this war effort or something criminal? Probably war effort, but I had better be alert" Peggy thought.

Leaving Richard's office, Peggy went to the production office to see when the parts might be ready for packaging. Bob Lord scratched his head, they were trying to build about 100 Beaufighter aircraft a year from three factories and a shadow engine factory in Lancashire. Another six which, from the order were urgently needed, would not be easy. He did have the bonus that the final assembly into an aircraft was not needed, but what was the level of sub-assembly needed?. "My best guess is the end of October, but someone else needs to do the boxes for every thing but the engines, as they arrive here in wooden boxes". Peggy noted the estimate and would make an entry in her diary for 20 October to check on progress. Bob set about changing the schedules and ordering extra raw components for the next batch.

Richard Davis saw Peggy returning from Bob's office and carefully replaced his telephone receiver. The man to whom he had been speaking had made it very clear that not only was Richard not to tell Peggy what the order was about, but he was also to tell her to make sure the transportation boxes looked like "non-military" products. Richard tried to work out how he could tell an intelligent and thoughtful worker to do something completely "out of the normal" without explaining why. "Well that is a problem for tomorrow" he thought. As she entered the area Peggy saw Richard almost secretively replacing his telephone. He looked worried and was clearly hiding something.

Having scribbled a note in her diary for 20 October, Peggy was next focussed on the scheduled deliveries for the coming week. "Something is not right here" she continued to think when she had time to think. These thoughts were reinforced when, on her way out of the factory that night, the gate guards were doing extra checks on identity documents, ladies handbags and coat pockets. The guard had simply said "routine random check" when she had asked the reasons for the extra checks.

On the bus to the bottom of the road to her parents and her home, she ended up sitting next to Colin Robinson a twenty five year old City of Bristol constable on his way to work. They had met at a dance and had sort of dated at a couple of dances, Colin knew he would be called up soon so did not want to get ‘serious’. In answer to Peggy's comments or maybe questions “Extra security tonight Robbo, I wonder what that was all about?” she said. “Reports of factory items being stolen or it could be spies” I would guess", Robbo had replied.

“Theft or spies, what is Richard mixed up in?” Peggy had thought.

The Shipment

It was September 1940. “Have you sorted the boxes for the six aircraft component order?” Richard asked Peggy. Sensing a chance to find out what was going on, Peggy said “No. I do not have any details of what to put on the packing? Richard seemed evasive “ I just need to know when the order will be ready to be moved. So when will we be ready, no delays?”. Peggy offered that Bob had said that the engines came ready boxed, so all we will need to do is to add the necessary markings. Peggy added that Bob had already sorted the extra boxes to be sent empty to Lancashire.” Peggy was hoping that the answers were sufficient to lever extra information from Richard.

Richard grunted, but said nothing. “Bob has said that war shortages mean that a full six aircraft will delay the planned deliveries to the Air Force” Peggy added. “Well Peg” Richard immediately stopped knowing that Peggy hated, with a vigour, having her name shortened. “Sorry Peggy, I think we might have that requirement slackened.” Desperate to avoid the tirade his mistake might unleash, Richard wanted to offer a win. “We could say the whole wings or fuselage sections are not needed, we need simply the components spares, sheets of skin metal” Richard added.

Peggy was now confused. “Richard is changing the order, how can he do this, that’s normally the Ministry only” she thought. “This is very odd: maybe this order is nothing to do with the Ministry" Her thoughts continued. Remembering Robbo's comments, Peggy mused "Are these parts not supporting the war effort at all? What should I do? I had better not show that I am concerned" Her thought process concluded. " Well I think that would ease Bob's life" Peggy said "and your apology is accepted" she added with a pointed voice. "Better show my usual anger" Peggy had thought.

Peggy returned to her office via Bob's, where she gave him the "good news" that the Ministry order requirement might be relaxed. Bob thought that the change could help, particularly if he interpreted it fairly liberally. Bob said that his team were not making much headway on getting suitable boxes for the parts to be transported to where-ever they were going. Peggy thought that this might be a way to ask questions of Richard so she said, “if you let me have the drawings I will try to get them made by local carpenters.”

The drawings were with her three days later. They had been clearly altered to be smaller than those originally drawn, but still large. Some were true boxes with the sides solid, but others had open sides “probably for large components e.g elevators” Peggy thought. Some of the open sided crates did not appear to have space to write or stencil a delivery address she noted.

She contacted some local carpenters she knew. How did she know them? Her younger sister had started a relationship with a young man completing his carpentry apprenticeship. So, as chaperone, she had met some of Betty’s young man's fellow carpenter’s. Most had been conscripted, including Betty's beau, but Peggy did manage to make contact with one or two and through them the business owners. She was generally met with the same response: "Yes we can make them, but getting the wood is the problem; there is war on you know".

Peggy later admitted to her mother that after the third 'There's a war" comment and Richard's secretiveness about this order "She lost it". Slamming the phone down, Peggy stormed down the corridor and marching straight past Richard's secretary, opened the door to his office. Not seeing the two men sat at the table behind the door, Peggy demanded to know " what is this special Beaufighter order really about?. "And you had better tell me the truth or I am going to the Police" she added with temper spilling from every word.

Richard's face coloured and he stammered "perhaps Mr Simmonds or Mr Hardcastle from the Air Ministry might explain". Still not seeing the two men at the table, Peggy responded " If you think I am going to listen to some fiction from an actor or traitor you must be stupid." Her anger was partly due to the problem of getting boxes made, but more from the thought that had grown in her recently that Richard was a traitor. So she was spitting out every word slowly and forcefully.

"We need to explain" a voice behind her said. Spinning round, Peggy saw two suited men sat at the work table behind the door. Without giving Peggy room to fire venomous words at them, Chris Simmonds (actually from the Churchill's war strategy team) said "Peggy what we are about to tell you is very sensitive to our long term success in this bitter struggle against Germany." "After we finish you will be required to sign the Official Secrets Act, divulging what we tell you will, I guarantee, put you in prison for a very long time." Peggy, embarrassed, confused but still angry nodded to indicate she understood, whether she would believe them was another matter.

Michael Hardcastle, a thin, grey haired weasel of a man started the explanation. "Success in this conflict will not be quick, we need to build our fight back capability. We need help and supplies, from our Commonwealth partners. To do this we need to ensure that the sea routes to America and India in particular remain open. In the case of India routes both around Africa and through the Suez Canal must remain open to us. To do this we are deploying the Navy and aircraft to our African friends. We also need to be able to service and repair these aircraft. To do this we are setting up a facility in South Africa. This order is to give the facility some start-up spares." Hardcastle stopped at this point for Peggy to absorb what she had been told.

Anger takes time to dissipate. Peggy's anger was banging around in her head. "Was this simply a prearranged cover story or was it true?" "Surely Richard could have said something earlier". "Why did he not stop me when I burst into his office?" "Why were these men here anyway? "That Hardcastle looks a crook"; were just some of the thoughts that spun around Peggy's thought processes.

As if reading her mind, Chris Simmonds said " We are here today to try to work out how to get the spares to South Africa in the most covert way possible". "We think an approach of hiding in clear sight is the best way" he added. Gathering some of her composure Peggy asked " What do you mean?" " Label them as Farm spares and send them via Bristol docks on one of the freighters en-route to India" was the response from Chris Simmonds.

Peggy thought for a minute and not wanting to be in the room any longer said "Well this is not something I know about, so I will leave you to it. Mr Davis, if could let me know how you want the shipment labelled I will get it done." As she turned to leave, Hardcastle piped up " Can you sign these forms before you go". waving the Official Secrets form in the air. Peggy did as she was asked and left the room with a piece of paper that might send her to prison at any time.

Back in her office she phoned the carpenter to make sure all the boxes had solid sides. If what she had been told was true, being able to see contents of the boxes would not be acceptable.

The boxes were eventually ready at the start of December. Late, because the air raids, shortages and the impossibility of what had been needed had combined to make the carpenter's life difficult to say the least.

Seventy-two boxes of various sizes, each with a serial number and labelled “Farm Spares” sat in Hanger 12 at the Bristol Aircraft Facility, Filton, awaiting collection. Peggy slipped a note inside two of the boxes (Boxes 12 and 31). It read “You are not forgotten, what you are doing is important. Stay safe and come home in the fullness of time.” Why she did this was not really clear. Partly it was a message to far away servicemen that Bristol appreciated what they were doing, partly maybe, just frustration at the mess the whole thing had become.

On It's Way

Bob Lord was pleased to see the fleet of lorries leave hanger 12. First, it gave him back a hanger for finishing. Second, it removed the need to stop pinching parts that were supposed to support finishing 'whole' aircraft and third, it would eventually mean the end of the need to answer questions about why parts were being sent to hanger 12; "when we are up against it to deliver aircraft to the forces". It did not help that the boxes the parts were going into were completely unlabelled which meant all sorts of rumours circulated within the factory. Unlabelled that was until early in the morning of the day of despatch when a thin, grey haired weasel of a man arrived at hanger 12 with stencils and black paint. He demanded total privacy and that no one should enter the hanger until the lorries arrived to move the boxes.

Peggy had seen the lorries arrive and be shepherded into the hanger by the thin, grey haired weaselly man. The sooner this was over the better she thought. War created enough uncertainty without this cloak-and-dagger stuff she thought. The boxes, including boxes 12 and 31 that contained the notes, were loaded by a crew that had come with the lorries. Peggy wondered who, if any one, would find the notes.

It was just before the lunch hooter when the first lorry emerged from the hanger, the last left as Peggy sat on a low wall in front of hanger 10, her usual place to eat the sandwich which her mum had prepared. Dad was a good gardener so the sandwich contained fresh carrot and cabbage with a thin spread of something meaty. She did not like the sandwich, the same as she had had for the last five working days, but they were fresh and tasty, just not a taste she enjoyed. As she sat on the wall Sarah Jones sat beside her. Her lunch was apple and a small piece of cheese, "the benefit of having a grocer as a dad" Peggy thought.

They discussed the recent bombing, which areas were badly damaged and how pleased they were that their houses had been spared. They also reviewed war news or at least what passed for news, most being rumour and guess-work. Eventually Sarah said that she had travelled in with John Gravel, who's son was the carpenter that Peggy's sister had been a "bit keen on". Sarah said that John was distraught because his son had been killed in a road accident caused by the black-out. Peggy froze, this news was terrible. The way things were this meant that she would have to break the news to Betty that night.

In fact Betty took the news fairly calmly, it appeared that she had enjoyed Graham Gravel's company, but it was not really serious. Whimsically Betty had said that it was more the smell of shaven wood than Graham himself.

The fleet of lorries made their way to Avonmouth docks, damage from the three days of bombing meant that they took various routes. Some even had to reverse because roads were blocked. Eventually, just before seven pm the last lorry arrived at shed three. Those lorries still laden at seven thirty were left loaded until the morning, previously the workers would have stayed until all were unloaded, but now most dockworkers simply wanted to get home. This shipment was not due to be loaded to the freighter for two or three days so the foremen let the workers go: primarily because the foremen wanted to go as well.

That night Ron was 'sleeping' in his bunk, Arabis had been submarine hunting off the Scilly Islands. Ron had actually done some electrical circuit work, which was satisfying. He had done his turn on deck looking for the tail-tail signs of the "silent" killers, but nothing had been seen. The ship suddenly healed over and sped up. Clearly some thing was a-foot. Expecting a call to action "stations" Ron rolled out of his bunk and sat on the edge of the bed structure next to Stan. No call came, so after about twenty minutes they returned to their bunks, they slept fitfully, waiting to be called back to duty.

The course change was real, The ship had been ordered to refuel and then to stand-by at the entrance to the Bristol Channel to escort a small convoy; destination India, precise harbour not given. The bridge was alive with officers planning routes, calculating fuel.

Cranes

The following morning at about eight in the morning a rather indistinct freighter tied up at berth 23 and started to “bunker” fuel oil. Reg and the Berth Freight Handling crew were told to load about 50 crates from shed 2 and the load that had arrived late the day before from shed 3. Reg and the crew inspected the freight to be loaded. Whilst everything in dock operations was signed for and signed for again, Reg had always marked some items in the load with his initials. For him it was a way of knowing what he had handled. In shed three they stood and looked at some crates marked “Farm Spares”. Harry Clarke was stood by some other crates, also marked “Farm Spares”, but he could also just make out fainter markings "Engine Assembly". Noting the destination as Cape Town, he called out: "They must have some almighty tractors down there. With these engines they must be able to plough the whole savanna in a day". " No" said Reg " they must need this power to out run the wild life". As the laughter died down Reg marked, at random two boxes: boxes 12 and 31.

Loading of the freighter took most of the day. Just as it was getting dark a thin, grey haired weasel of a man arrived and checked both the crane log and the ships manifest. The air raid warning sounded and as before, Reg was down the ladder in minutes and running towards the air raid shelter: this time remembering to set all the switches and levers to safe. Welsh Jones checked him in and Reg again sat about half way down the shelter. The bombs seemed closer, they were louder and the shelter seemed to shake from time to time. Suddenly there was a resounding bang and the sound of grinding metal. The silence followed by a noise which Reg could never really describe. The far end of the shelter became a cloud of dust, men shouting and shards of metal clattering to the floor.

"What the hell has happened down there" Welsh Jones yelled. He was pushing his way past startled dock workers. Reg joined him. As they got closer it was clear that some thing heavy had fallen onto the shelter. The shelter had dealt with most of the force, but the dust deposited since construction had been dislodged and where men had been sitting the buckling roof and sides had caused minor injuries and, eventually, head aches for some. Reg stared at some metal poking through the wall. “This looks like crane ten” Reg said. Someone shouted ”That bugger Hitler has a meaningful hit”. “ Nah, I told the gaffer before that the legs were rusting through. I reckon it has given up the ghost” another added. Welsh Jones, with surprising skill for one thought "not to have the skills to tick a list correctly”, dealt with the injured and organised a cleaning and shoring up operation.

When the raid was over the workers poured out of the shelter to better inspect the wreckage. Yes it was crane ten and yes, even in the torchlight rust was probably the cause. The night made for a set of good war stories for many once D-Day arrived. The variety of stories was startling: many injuries, hardening he-men actions to save lives, widespread devastation, Reg heard many versions of that night retold by families not realising that Reg had been there.

Just as the crane was crashing to the ground, Ron was watching the shadow of Plymouth disappear. The ship swung west-ward and through the night zig-zagged its way to the round the Lizard and by daylight reached the entry to the Bristol Channel, where it steered an aimless course, clearly waiting for orders or something else. Ron and the rest of the crew did their shifts or were on deck searching the sea for the enemy submarines. Most slept poorly, what would tomorrow bring?

The following day, the crew on the bridge of the Arabis saw three merchant vessels steaming towards them. They had formed the flotilla as they came down the Channel. Two, including the one Reg had loaded came from Avonmouth and one from Cardiff. Using lights rather than radio, the corvette and the merchant ships identified themselves and established a formation. Arabis was joined late in the afternoon by two other corvettes, HMS Camellia and HMS Clematis, Just as dusk was forming three more merchant ships and their escort joined, having sailed down the Irish Sea from Liverpool. With the four corvettes essentially at the North, South, East and West of the six merchant ships, the convey started into the area considered by the U-Boat captains as “good hunting grounds”.

As Ron and Stan sat on their bunks, the general opinion was that this small convoy was on its way to Halifax, but the “Old Sweats” i.e. had been in the Navy for 6 months longer than most, said that they were already too far South, “more likely Gibraltar”, was their best guess. The actually declared destination of India never entered their minds. And they certainly never considered Cape Town as a first delivery destination.

All at Sea

The next morning there was no electrical work for Ron, so after some training time and some gauge watching, it was "on deck" watching for the dreaded signs of a U-boat. Eyes not watching the sea surface, Ron raised his gaze to the convoy. He saw that one of the corvettes was no longer in sight.

The remaining three corvettes had essentially divided the convoy into 120 degree segments. Each boat moving within the 120 segment to try to ensure the search area was as wide as possible.

Under the surface the crew of the U-boat tensed as the boat slowly rose to periscope height. It was near the end of the patrol. It had not been a very fruitful patrol and the commander feared the reaction from the hierarchy on his return to port.

A short sweep of the periscope, maybe less than 5 to 6 degrees and he saw a merchant vessel, a few minutes more and he could see 3 more. His excitement rose and training disappeared. Ordering the periscope down he gathered his second in command and explained what he had seen. The second in command said that they had had a signal to seek and destroy a small convoy (four to eight ships) heading south into the Bay of Biscay. This convoy would not be following the usual Atlantic route. It was considered a high value target. The commander saw that a successful attack would turn the patrol into a great contribution to the war effort.

The two of them gathered all the information they could. Plotted the course they estimated that the convoy was taking and then set about planning an attack strategy. They wanted to sink at least two of the merchant ships: all three would be exceptional. They estimated that any escorts were at the four corners of the convoy and not expecting an attack.

For the next hour the submarine commander moved around the convoy, checking positions and course. Not wishing to give the escorts the opportunity to detect their presence, periscope use was limited to a few seconds, essentially looking in the direction they expected to see the convoy. Twice the positions of two of the freighters would have made it possible to fire on both from the same point. The commander's mind raced: he would be a hero.

Just before mid afternoon the commander, noting that they had been submerged for about 90 minutes and that the convoy was moving well away from the Atlantic routes, decided that it was time to attack. They would have the sun behind them, so no glare on the periscope picture. They would be about 4000 yards from the first target and about 5000 yards from the second. The ship was readied for action, normally they would have attacked at night while on the surface, but that was just not possible, so it was to be a near surface firing, followed by a turn and run for 20 minutes and then surface since they would have no battery power left!

Lining up on the convoy targets the U-Boat rose to be a point where the tower was just below the surface. “Loose, Loose, Loose, Loose” was the command. Immediately the submarine started to dive and turn tail. The torpedos were on their way. The intended targets, the merchant ship with the "Farm spares" and one with scrap metal to become the much needed steel, apparently totally unaware of their impending destruction.

The radio operator on Arabis shouted into the microphone “Break. Break. Break”. On board the merchant ships wheel men became busy changing the headings of their ships. Arabis itself was turning sharply and was, clearly to all those onboard, accelerating to maximum speed. “Action stations”, Depth charges flying left and right of the ship. Ron stared at “his bit of the sea” expecting to see tail-tail bubbles of a torpedo ripping towards them. No matter how hard he starred; no sign. Time was standing still as they waited for the inevitable.

From nowhere Clematis hammered past them on a reverse heading to Arabis. As soon as she passed a volley of depth charges poured from the corvette. Arabis continued to turn and then, almost as quickly, reversed heading to make towards the disappearing merchant ships. Clearly it was the role of Clematis to chase the U-boat.

The volley of torpedos were in-front of Arabis, had she turned earlier she would have been hit, possibly fatally. Having missed Arabis the torpedos plowed towards the merchant ships. The “Break” radio message prompted a course change that put both merchant ships running parallel to the torpedo tracks. One pair raced past the side of one of the merchant ships and ran out of battery power before reaching the second ship. The other pair reached their target one banged into the rudder but failed to explode, the other simply did not trigger. This merchant ship slowed a little whilst the crew tried to understand if there had been any effect on the ship.

Aboard the U-Boat the depth charges banged and shook the boat. As it dived the vibrations became more severe. The crew worried that the hull would not withstand the over pressures, but fortunately the dive was keeping the submarine ahead of the sinking charges. They survived, levelled out and ran for 15 minutes, cut the engines and slowly rose to the surface. At periscope height the commander did a 360 degree sweep: how he wished he had done this before he attacked. Clematis was turning back towards the convey. The submarine surfaced, opened hatches to purge the stale air and ran the engines to recharge the batteries. Both gun crews on the submarine and Clematis saw each others shapes, but neither ship engaged: Clematis because protection being a higher priority than submarine destruction and the U-boat because engagement would also certainly result in destruction, a resource Germany could not afford to lose.

The commander knew it was time to return to base, to face the music: the patrol was a failure, but it could have been different. How he wished that the sinking of merchant ships would be confirmed later.

So how was it that the attack was so well repelled? Stan aboard Arabis, had seen the trail of the periscope as it had disappeared on the first U-boat contact with the convoy. The first officer had reacted to Stan's sighting, the only one on the ship; without question. Guessing what the U-Boat commander might do. He had assumed that attack would be with the sun behind the submarine and that it would be within an hour of the sighting. With the Captain's agreement they maintained their course to convince the submarine crew that it's presence had not been detected. They signalled the merchant ships with courses to be set at the "break" command; courses designed to minimise the profile of the ships relative to the torpedo's track. Next Clematis was positioned to make an attack assuming Arabis would cut across the submarines attack direction. Little did they know how accurately they would guess the attack time and direction. Finally, the deck crews on Arabis detected the attack the instant the periscope broke the surface: pure luck, but much appreciated by all.

Ron:
Between the Lines

The convoy continued to make its way towards the West African coast. The seas were rough. Some crew members on each of the ships were sea-sick. The merchant ship that had been hit by the torpedo seemed little damaged although changing direction was a slower affair. Arabis had been signalled to press on and not to allow the ship to "put in" for repairs.

On day three of the convoy one of the merchant vessels signalled to the Arabis that they had a serious electrical fault and that their electrician was so ill that he could not be used to fix the fault. The fault was in one of the systems that measured fuel flow and this would affect the convoy speed. The convoy speed was already too slow for the captain of Arabis. An increased slowness increased substantially their vulnerability to aerial or seaborne attack. He did not know that there were no German resources anywhere near them.

The discussion with his first officer was short and functional. The convoy had to continue, slowing was not an option. No, they were not going to send their best (full-time) naval electricians; how about one of the conscripts? Ron was considered the best at understanding systems. The sea was too rough for a Liberty boat transfer, so it would have to be by Breeches Buoy. So this is how Ron's Breeches Buoy "trip" came about.

Ron looked on in horror as he was told his fate and what it entailed. His pride that he had not joined the mass ranks of the sea-sick disappeared as his stomach deposited breakfast at the thought of being "swung" from the corvette to the merchant ship. He just missed the Chief Sparks' boots, but it was damn close!

An hour later Ron was on deck to watch the corvette crew fire the initial connection to the merchant ship. If only the crews had practised the process, Ron would have had greater confidence. Just as the pistol was fired Arabis lurched on the swell, so instead of the shot scribing a neat, flattish arch to the waiting crew on the merchant ship, the pistol shot ballooned over the merchant ship bridge. Crew scrambled over superstructure and gang-ways to grab the thin line before it either entangled essential systems or fell back into the sea. Finally the initial cable was captured and the Arabis crew began to payout the main Breeches Buoy cable and the pulley cable. Eventually the cables were hauled aboard the merchant ship and made fast against the bridge structure. The anchor point was rusted and paint flaked from the surrounding areas. To Ron the sea swell seemed to be strengthening.

The chief of deck crew said: " Ron have you got all the tools you need in the sack? the sack was tied to his waist". "Yes, Sir" Ron replied. "Get into the harness lad" was the next command. Ron, was now standing on a low profile deck housing. He stepped into the harness, which was connected to a pulley. The pulley hung on the cable with one smaller cable stretching out to the merchant ship and a second held by the Arabis deck crew. "Ready?", it was not really a request, it was a command. As the two ships adjusted their tracks to tension the pulley cable, Ron shot upwards as the main cable between the ships tensioned. The deck crew waved to the merchant man to start pulling. Ron jerked forward.

For a few minutes all went well and Ron, dangling from the cable, edged over the side of Arabis and moved towards the merchant ship. Unfortunately the damage to the rudder of the merchant ship meant that it could not, in the swell, maintain it's course relative to Arabis. The ships closed in on each other, tension in the cable was lost: Ron plunged towards the sea. Training was that in such an event the crew of the ship to which Ron was nearest would pull him in and the other crew would release. Unfortunately crew training was not that good, both crews thought they should pull. A tug-of-war developed with Ron getting closer and closer to being dunked into the cold sea.

Officers commanding the deck crews, at the same time, identified the problem and in unison issued a "stop pulling" command. Both sides of the pulley cables went slack. Ron, as a result, continued downwards to, what he was now sure, would be his watery grave. Suddenly the commands to the merchant ship rudder took effect such that it's course became divergent from the corvette. The pulley cable suddenly became taut, firing Ron upwards, but only after the harness had cut firmly into his groin and the tool sack broke free from his belt to swing on the lanyard keeping it attached to his belt. Seeing the change, the Arabis crew responded by pulling him in. With no tension on the pulley from the merchant ship Ron shot towards the corvette: the tool sack, responding to Ron's change of direction, swung round and it was at this point Ron realised that putting a four pound hammer in the sack was a poor decision, the sack with the hammer arched round and smashed him in the midriff. Ron's motion caused the corvette crew to lose control of their pulley cable, just as the merchant ship crew, slower to react, now pulled the Breeches Buoy cable towards them. Ron was now heading towards the merchant ship and yes, the tool sack was now swinging the other way around into his body to deliver a second blow to his midriff.

It would be nice to note that the situation stabilised. But it did not. Now Ron is heading upwards and towards the merchant ship. The swell and the limited effect of the merchant ships rudder meant that the cable went slack again. Ron passes the pulley; he is going up and the pulley down. The harness tightens and Ron stops going up and reverses direction. If only someone had told the tool sack. This continues upwards until the lanyard tightens, the sack swings over Ron's shoulder and delivers a blow to his back. Now going back towards the sea Ron prepared himself for an inevitable dunking. But no, the ships retighten the cable; this arrested the downward motion, again exerting pain on Ron's groin. Shortly afterwards the tool sack makes another impact with Ron's body. This sequence of down, up, backwards and forwards, tool sack blows to midriff, shoulder, knees lasted for three more cycles. Eventually the merchant ship crew won the day and Ron, exhausted, bruised, sick, wet and angry banged into the hull on the merchant ship and was dragged aboard. Every one involved in the transfer agreed that it had been far less than text book perfect.

Taken below, Ron was given a hot drink, some ill fitting clothes while the merchant ship crew dried his fatigues and given an hour to recover. He later diagnosed the problem with the freighter's electrics and rigged a fix. At which time there was agreement that a reverse transfer to Arabis was ill advised, particularly for Ron's sanity. Ron was to stay onboard until they next docked.

Life aboard the merchant ship was relatively easy particularly once the crew electrician recovered. The systems were generally robust and apart from some routine checks, most of the time was "on deck" watching the sea go by. To relieve the boredom, Ron "inspected" all areas of the ship, including the holds. In the holds he saw crates and crates of "Farm Spares". Two of the crates carried the stencilled initials “RGT”. Ron knew that these were the marks that his brother Reg sometimes put on loads he had handled. With no thought in particular, using his pen knife Ron carved “RFT” his initials, below Reg’s on boxes 12 and 31.

In Cape Town, which was the next port, Ron rejoined Arabis. Arabis did not travel to India with the convoy, instead the ship returned to Plymouth.

Les

At the same time that Peggy was dealing with the order for the Beaufighters, Les had looked out of the troop ship port hole, along with 2000 others. It had not been an arduous trip, the ship had been about half full. Once the submarine threat in the South-West approaches and the Bay of Biscay had been passed through every thing had been relaxed. Clearly this war thing was not too bad. All would, in the fullness of time agree and once they forgot the hell of initial training, they had gotten away with it very lightly to start with.

Table Top Mountain was now clearly visible. For some there would be a long, long journey through Africa arriving to support the Suez Canal protection forces. For others they would eventually engage the enemy as part of the Desert campaign. A select few would stay for some time in South Africa. Les was one of the fortunate few.

Fred and Nelly's third child Les was born in 1921. A child who was good with his hands and not bad with books or sport; he was destined to achieve a sound, all round school experience. Les, whilst he might have wanted to “stay on” at school, because the family finances dictated that he left at 14, entered an apprenticeship for cabinet making. He did night school, so by the time he had his indentures, not only could he build his own and the family's furniture, he could also draw plans that could pass local authority planning requirements.

At the time neither Les nor the others had any idea why they were on their way to Africa. Many years afterwards Les had reasoned that "clearly, someone with sense in the war office saw that a carpenter who could read plans was ideally suited to construct and repair the Allies wooden and metal aircraft in South Africa". So that was that.

Some basic training, mostly (and a lot of) marching about, cleaning boots and learning how to bandage a wound (badly) and then a sea voyage from Southampton via Lisbon meant that his war started in Africa as an aircraft "mechanic"; although he really knew nothing about aircraft.

Les was not the only one to be held back at the dock side. Some 60 other "tradesmen" were all there to "service" UK and US /Canada manufactured aircraft. From disembarking the troop carrier, they had shuffled through arrival checks (exactly the same as those for boarding) "Do they think we somehow transformed on the trip" one tired voice called out."You did Kevin, you put on ten stone on all that ships food" another called out. Clearing the arrival checks they climbed aboard Army trucks that rushed them through the city and out into rough scrub land and eventually towards what looked like a deserted army training ground: no longer needed by anyone and certainly, to everyone's view, not intrinsic to winning the war in Africa or anywhere.

They disembarked the trucks, grabbed their kit bags. The trucks drove away. "Where are they going?" a Norfolk accent called out. "Norwich", a sarcastic voice replied. The disappearing lorries worried Les, were they being abandoned? He need not have worried the lorries belonged to a transport corp camped about 3 kilometres away in a wood to make it difficult for prying eyes to know what was happening.

As the trucks disappeared the men were instructed to form into company lines. A drill sergeant called them to "dress right". Clearly training lessons had been clouded by the voyage as the lines could best be described as ragged. The drill sergeant started to turn red as he witnessed what could be only described as a tea room dance as each man realigned himself with the next on the right, unfortunately this man was moving as well. It might have stabilised if the right most man in each line had stood still, but he was convinced that he had to be in line with the man on his left. To add to the effect, rather than take two small shuffle-like steps as taught in training, the right markers were taking near full strides each time they moved. This then was replicated as others sought to realign themselves. Six lines of human serpents gyrated about the parade ground for some 5 or 6 minutes. The drill sergeant, absolutely purple by now, simply yelled “stand still”: not a known parade square command to many, to try to stop the fiasco. Private Jones, who became known as Private Grimace, proved to be the solution. The drill sergeant simply stamped on the foot of the right most man in the front row, pinning his foot to the ground. Hence Private Grimace: simply the expression on Private Jones face as the drill sergeant maintained downward pressure on his foot. Taff Jones became Private Grimace for the rest of the war. Slowly the serpents wriggled to a stand still. Straight, the lines were not.

Recognising the right marker problem the drill sergeant marched the width of the parade square and without ceremony dragged each of the remaining five lines right most individual into position. These were then told to “Stand still”, although the instruction had been preceded with a venomous swear word. Terror prevailed and the six stood very still while the lines finally tea-danced themselves into almost straight lines. Not the military's finest moment all there would agree.

A Royal Engineers Major stepped forward to address the “lines”. Not realising how loud the collective sigh would be, the Major issued the “stand-easy” command. The clatter of dropped equipment on this command was, what he wrote later in his diary, “staggering and frightening”. This team were in South Africa to turn the aged facility into an aircraft maintenance outpost. Much later in the conflict, the Major confided to Les that what he had seen was

"Frightening because of what had to be done, the standard to be achieved and the impossible time scale. The Major had told Les that he wrote is his diary that "this lot cannot even parade properly, so how on earth can we build a servicing facility in six weeks?".

The initial tasks were to pitch tents, dig latrines and erect a mess tent. Sunset saw all this achieved and the men fed. Some of the tents did leave a lot to be desired: missing poles, strings that had been broken and then granny-knotted together. They were all lined up, but only because the drill sergeant's team were sent out with marker poles!

Les was in the corner of a 4 man tent. They were all carpenters, exhausted and bemused. The meal could best be assessed as filling, but it did not matter, sleep came within 10 minutes of laying down on the camp-beds. This would be Les' home for the next 2 years.

South Africa

The next six weeks had the carpenter's key building skills exercised to the full as wooden framed buildings some, those more vital to success, were given a cladding of either local bricks or sheet metal; what ever could be found. Les enjoyed the carpentry, but the military bit: parades, boot and kit cleaning etc could be “parked”.

The base was ready a few days before the first aircraft were due to arrive so the men were given some time to relax. A trip to Table Top Mountain, not the intended destination, but the corporal in charge of the "outing" was not the best map reader in the world. During the "tour" the truck full of men, including Les came upon a brightly coloured snake by the side of the road. The truck stopped for the men to observe the snake, the species of which no one had any idea. The men, to a man, jumped as it awoke and decided to slither down the road. Army men being what they are, the call was made for the truck to move and keep pace and the driver, sensing fun, obliged.

With men shouting encouragement the truck gained speed and caught up with the snake. At this time the men started to offer identification of the snake. "Cobra", "Anaconda", "Viper" were obvious, repeated, but wrong. "Yellow Tree Snake" was offered by one who had seen a Tree Snake in a Zoo. He was not confident in this definition, partly because the one he had seen was not yellow! The snake's speed prompted an offer of "African Leopard Snake", on advice updated to "African Cheetah Snake". Clearly none of them were snake experts.

The snake could either have thought is was under attack or just for the "hell of it" accelerated away from the truck: this was not a new truck, it had seen better days and sad to say the snake won, the truck retired with steam hissing from the radiator. The damage meant that they missed any further "safari" experience that day; mind you the speed of the snake convinced most that visiting any element of the country-side was a very, very bad idea. Whilst returning to camp they made an unplanned visit to the base of Table Top Mountain. Les always intended to get to the top, but never did.

The aircraft arrived and the airforce conscripts undertook servicing. Les and the other tradesmen thought that the servicing was just like a car: fill up with water, oil and fuel, kick the tyres and polish anything that looked as though it needed a polish. The reason for this was that they did not have any spares so repairs or replacement was simply not on the "work plan".

The convoy carrying the ‘Farm Spares’ made it into port a day or two after the first aircraft arrived. The transport team eventually delivered the crates. The crates were deposited in an empty shed. Since most of the crates were wooden the obvious decision was to appoint carpenters to open the crates and transport the parts to the ‘stores’ in another shed, but at least this one was water tight against the tropical rain.

Les was one of those opening crates. He was allocated crate four. It was relatively straight forward to open as it was an entire engine assembly, quickly whisked away by the "stacking" team.

The next crate for Les was number twelve. As he approached it he did not see the markings, it was only as he unscrewed the lid that he saw the initials stencilled and carved. The sight brought a lump to his throat. In the still of his bunk he often thought about his family and hoped that all were well: to see these initials confirmed they (or at least Reg and Ron) were still alive. After a few minutes quite contemplation Les broke the crate down and placed the spares ready for collection. Just as he gathered up the wood (to be used for shelves, bed repairs etc) he saw a piece of paper. He picked it up and read it, firstly to himself and then, after he had composed himself, to those in the shed.

Les announced: "Chaps I have found this message in one of the crates." He read: "You are not forgotten, what you are doing is important. Stay safe and come home in the fullness of time". Those in the shed warmed to the words and for the rest of the day were on a high. The similar note in Crate 31 made its way to the aircraft engine mechanics and then to the aircrew.

What happened to the note in crate 31 is not known. The one in crate 12 went into Les' back pocket, then into his kit pack and 4 years later in to his demob suit. Les had offered the note to others, but most thought as he found it he should keep it.

Les never found another crate with initials nor letters, although he did look carefully at every crate that arrived from England.

He kept the piece of wood with his brother's marks for all the time he was in South Africa. It mainly propped one of the legs of his bunk, occasionally making an appearance as a make-do cricket bat. Eventually wear and tear took its toll and it was neither a bat nor a support, so when Les and company were moved on, the wood stayed behind: a sort of marker to the events and the time.

Epilogue

All the brothers, Doris and their parents survived the war. The family home, although rocked was never destroyed by bombs and was much the same when Ron and Les returned as it was when they had left. Reg and Nelly's son was an addition.

Reg had worked hard in the docks through out most of the early part of the conflict, but was later posted elsewhere in England as others were trained to operate the cranes. From the perspective of changing the direction of the war Reg was certain that the bombing had not been successful. Yes, Bristol was damaged, but generally the bombs created disruption rather than destruction. Lives were sadly lost, but not friends of the family. After the war Reg returned to the docks, but eventually left the docks to become a Pub Landlord. Much appreciated by the band of serious drinkers whom he inherited when he took over at each of his pubs.

When Arabis returned to Plymouth, Ron was reassigned to training for loading ammunition and then to aircraft carriers, so at least he was working with aircraft. Ron completed numerous Atlantic runs on various ships. He was always worried about surviving, but was also philosophical "If someone had to do it, it might as well be him". He was pleased he never did another Breeches Buoy ship to ship transfer. Once the war in Europe was completed his ship was on its way to Japan. The announcement of the end of war with Japan over the ships tannoy system was met with an immediate reverse of course and cheers from the whole crew. As they passed through the Red Sea many of the crew celebrated peace by leaping into the sea from the flight deck: it was just as well the “old man” cut the engines and launched the Liberty boats to collect the celebrants, otherwise there could have been some “lost in action” reports. Ron qualified as an electrician and spent many years fitting out shops and new houses.

Les had over two years in South Africa repairing aircraft. He then moved to Egypt and finally repatriated through Gibraltar. Once repatriated Les went back to his carpentry skills. The brothers all remembered demobbed servicemen camped at Eastville "park' or common, depending on which one did the remembering, but all were thankful that they had the family home to which they could return. Each felt fortunate that they had been able to restart their pre-war careers.

Les in the less hectic times in Africa had studied the note from crate 12. He knew two things. It had been signed by a "Peggy" and it was probably put in the crate just before the crate was sealed. Reg had remembered that some of the lorries that delivered the crates came from the Bristol Aircraft Company. Les knew some of the apprentices working there and so eventually he found out who the "Peggy" was, even better: he found out where she lived, just two streets and about half a mile from his parents home.

Just wanting to let her know that the note was appreciated by all those working at the maintenance airfield and to say thank you, one winter's evening he walked to the address for Peggy and knocked on the door. Lucky for him Peggy answered. After some awkward exchanges, primarily because Peggy had forgotten the letter in all the mayhem that had followed the shipping of the parts, she invited him in for tea.

Her parents were out at some meeting. Sitting round the fire were Peggy's boyfriend and her sister Betty. It must have been the smell of newly turned wood on Les' clothes that meant he soon had a date with Betty.

They married 1947.

Acknowledgements

I need to acknowledge the considerable support I had in bringing these stories together from my sister Lynne and brother David and from my cousin Tim. Without their input valuable additional material might well have been lost.

To friends and relatives who took the time to proof read and critique, thank you

Equally valuable, has been the encouragement from my wife Theresa. Without her continuous support and insights this might never have been completed.

I have added a picture of my father and uncles some time after the war.

One nephew wanted to know what a Beau-fighter looked like, so I have added some pictures and a drawing.

The Brothers, some time after the war

Bristol Beaufighter in Flight 1940

Bristol Beaufighter Crew pose after flight 1941

Pen Drawing of the Bristol Beaufighter with an Early nose mounted Radar

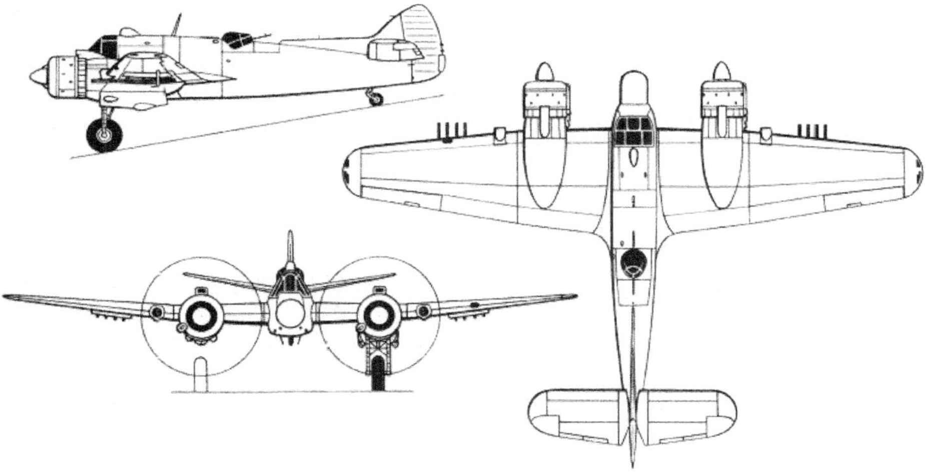

All aircraft pictures and drawings are courtesy of Royal Aeronautical Society Library

Printed in Great Britain
by Amazon

26919962R00066